CONTENTS

1. My Own Face   1

2. Deep Inside   6

3. Smiles with no End   17

4. Without any Fuss   24

5. So Far Away   34

6. Wake Up   38

7. In the Mirror   42

8. Do It Again   50

CHAPTER 1

My Own Face

MARIANNE

People come in and out of the room. I don't move so I can't always see where they are, but when someone comes up close in front of me then I can see them properly.

There's a woman with a fat little face and short black hair. She's always staring at me. For a while I thought she was looking at me, but in fact she is looking at herself. One time, she looked at me very close up. Then she turned round and spoke to someone else. "I look and look at her, but all I ever see is my own face," she said.

I don't know what I am.

Not a person.

Not a picture.

I must be something shiny.

A Christmas tree bauble, perhaps. A window. Or perhaps I'm a mirror.

The woman with the short black hair
is always holding things up in front of
me – a teddy bear, a CD, clothes, photos of
people. She talks a lot as she sits next to me,
although there's no one here to talk to. She's

looking for someone called Marianne. She calls for Marianne over and over again.

I'd like to tell her that Marianne isn't here. There's no one here. But I can't speak.

CHAPTER 2

Deep Inside

MUM

Hospitals have always made me stressed. All those ill people! I'm sure that if you go into a hospital you'll fall ill and die yourself.

I remember I went with my mother to a hospital when I was a child – we were visiting someone, I can't remember who. We walked past a sign that said – **Infectious diseases**.

I asked Mum what "infectious" meant and she told me.

"It means an illness other people can catch," she said.

'Oh!' I thought. 'I've gone past that sign so I might die.'

This hospital is different. It's not me that I'm scared for this time. Now I know that the worst things don't happen to you – they happen to your children. My husband said to me, "When the children bury the parents, that's natural. But when the parents bury the children, that's tragic."

Marianne is my child and she is already buried, deep inside herself where no one can dig her up.

*

The hospital is warm and smells of disinfectant and boiled cabbage – the smell of school meals. I trot down the corridor. I've been coming here for so long now that it doesn't feel strange any more. It's like a second home.

Sister Charlie is on duty. "Any change?" I ask.

"Just the same," the Sister says.

She leads the way to the room where Marianne lies. She opens the door and she smiles as she walks up to the bed.

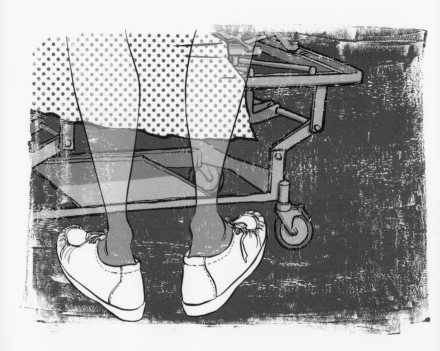

"Good colour today. Rosy cheeks! Nice and healthy," Sister Charlie says, with a smile for me.

It's true. Marianne's cheeks are flushed a bright, pretty pink, as if she's been out for a crisp walk.

"Well, I'll leave you to it," Sister Charlie says. "Cup of tea? Yes? I'll get one sent in. Good luck. Goodbye, Marianne."

Sister Charlie always says goodbye to Marianne like that. It's good manners. For a long time the doctors told us that it was possible that Marianne could hear every word anyone says. I don't think anyone believes that any more – not even me and her dad. But we have to be careful, just in case.

I put One Direction on the CD player. I'm teasing, of course. Marianne always loved to be teased, it used to make her shriek! If she were here now she'd shriek like a kettle.

"No, Mum," she'd say. "Not them. No one listens to them any more, you know that! And they were only ever for babies."

'Yes, but you used to, Marianne,' I think. 'Do you remember? You used to know every song backwards. You and Jess and Zara used to do the dance moves. It was only a few years ago, and already you think you were a baby then.'

I hold up the CD.

"Remember?" I ask her.

Marianne lies with her head pushed a little back into the pillow. Her eyes are half open, and her mouth is ajar like a door.

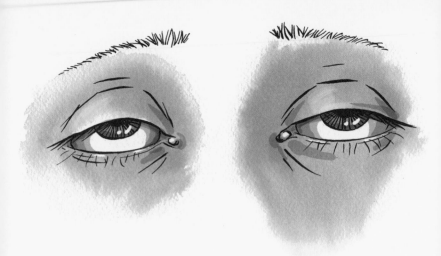

Tubes go into her mouth and up her nose.
She never moves.

"Remember?" I ask again. I hold her
hand. "Give a little squeeze if you can hear
me," I say.

I wait. It might take a long time for
her muscles to move. She has to find them

again. The doctors have said that. If she
ever comes back to us, it will start in a tiny
way – so little you might almost not notice
it. So I wait. I close my eyes. I try to feel
the slightest tiny pressure on my fingers, but
there's never any response.

"Remember," I beg. "Please, Marianne?
Can you hear me?"

Nothing. I bend and kiss her.

I would give everything I have for her to kiss me back.

I sit and wait for my tea, stroking her face, her arm, her hands.

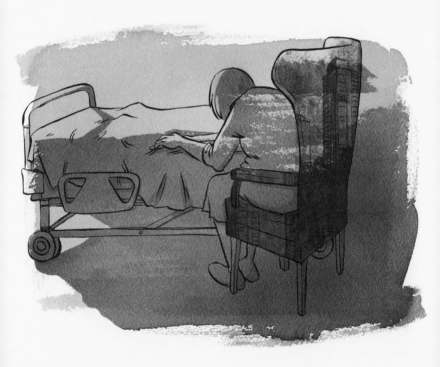

CHAPTER 3

Smiles with no End

MARIANNE

Today I had a memory.

It began with the woman, the sad one
with the short dark hair, who comes in every
day to stare at her own face in my eyes.

"Marianne, Marianne, can you hear me?" she pleads. "Can you hear me? Marianne, Marianne ..."

What does she want? Why can't she leave me alone?

I don't know who this Marianne person is – why does she keep calling me by her name? Perhaps she's teasing me. If I could, I'd block her out altogether. But it's nice to feel her warm breath on my face. She touches me with her cold hand. Sometimes she remembers to warm her hands on her breath before she touches my cheek. One

time, she put her head close to mine so our cheeks touched. She lay against me like that for so long that I think I fell asleep. That's when I had my memory.

This is my memory.

I was lost. I can't remember how I got lost. I think I'd just wandered away too far. I remember tall houses behind hedges. I remember the road. It was dark and speckled with little white and brown stones, and I had no idea how to get home.

Then I was in a house with some people who must have taken me in. One of them asked me if I wanted something to eat. I was hungry, but I was too shy to say yes. Then my mum came to fetch me, and I was so happy, so happy to see her.

I ran to her when she came into the room and flung my arms around her, and I can remember smiling and smiling and smiling at her, smiles with no end. I was so happy to have her back. She was trying to be cross but she was smiling too because I was so happy, and all the people in the room at the table were all smiling at me because I was so, so happy to have my mum back ...

Then I realised what all this is about.

You see, I was a person, too. Once upon a time. I was a girl called Marianne. I had a mother. The woman with the black hair – you see? She was my mother. I had a father too – the man she calls Aidan. He smells of smoke when he comes in with her sometimes. And who knows who else there was? Brothers and sisters and friends.

It was long ago. Then something happened. The woman, the mother, thinks that I'm still Marianne. Poor woman! I wish I could tell her that Marianne is gone. Once I was Marianne, but then something happened and I got turned into this instead.

CHAPTER 4

Without any Fuss

MUM

"I don't believe she's in any pain," Dr Morris says. Her voice is calm and kind.

I nod, but I can't get it out of my mind. What if Marianne's lying there in agony, day after day, week after week, month after month? And she can't say a word.

"The real question is not if she's in any pain, but whether or not she's ever going to wake up. It's been 8 months now," Dr Morris says. "Her body is healthy, but there's no sign of any person inside at all."

My Marianne. She's perfectly healthy but not a person.

Now the hospital has had enough. There are so many ill people and not enough staff, not enough beds, not enough doctors. Of course, my child has a right to life, but there is another choice. We can simply end the support. No drugs to kill her, but no medicines to fight off illness, and no food or water to keep her alive. They say they would keep her asleep, there would be no pain. Perhaps she can't even feel pain – none of us thinks so any more anyway. Marianne would pass away without any fuss or distress within a week.

Aidan squeezes my hand. We've talked about this before. We knew it would come. Probably it's the right thing to do.

Probably is a big word.

Aidan clears his throat. Doctor Morris looks up.

"What are the chances that she might come round after so long?" he wants to know.

"Very small." The doctor shakes her head. "Brain activity is very low. I would be very surprised if there was ever any improvement. In our opinion ..."

"In your opinion, she should die." My voice jars in the little still office. Doctor Morris closes her lips in a thin line.

"In my opinion, Marianne is already dead, Mrs Sims," she says. "At this stage, we're just telling you what we believe would be best. The decision is yours. I understand how painful this must be."

Aidan nods. "While there's life, there's hope," he says.

The doctor bows her head. "In this case, very little hope, I'm afraid."

"But there is some," I insist.

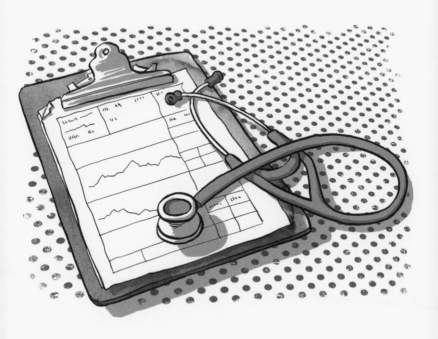

"Very little," she repeats.

Aidan and I nod, like dogs in the back of a car.

*

Aidan and I go into Marianne's room and watch her. Is that my daughter? Is there anyone here apart from us?

While there's life there's hope, but hope can be cruel. What about the rest of us? Our son, Rory. Poor child, he's had little enough of my time this past year. The strain is crushing us. Marianne is ruining our lives. The coma goes on and on and on. She's not my daughter any more. She is, to be very blunt, a vegetable.

I sit on the bed and hold up her things. Her little tank top.

"Do you remember, Marianne?" I say. "Nana bought you this. You wore it until it got so tight it looked daft and I had to hide it from you. Your necklace of wild pearls. Do you remember this, Marianne? Marianne? Marianne? Please wake up, darling."

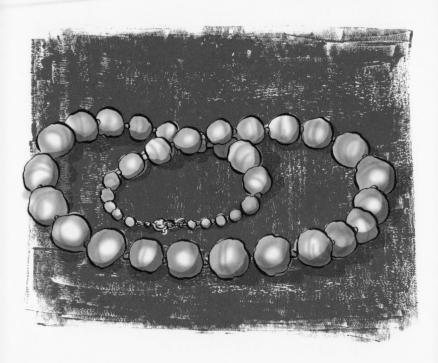

"Marianne, wake up, Marianne, wake up!"
I say again. "You have to wake up, darling,
please, it's getting very late. Marianne!"

Aidan takes my arm. I'm shouting.

"She can't hear you, Julie."

I stand up. I take a breath.

"We can't be sure," I tell him.

"We can never be sure. But." He looks at the floor.

"Give her another week. One week," I beg.

Aidan pauses. "A bit longer than that, perhaps. There's no hurry."

"We've waited this long," I say.

"It's her birthday next month," he says. "Let's wait for that."

CHAPTER 5

So Far Away

MARIANNE

Why one month? Why not two or three?
Why not for ever?

It's all so far, far away.

Mum? Are you still there? You see, I'd
like to come back, even if it's just to say
goodbye. But I can't quite make it.

I can remember a lot now.

I can remember her, my mother. I can remember my father and Rory, and my friends. I remember the music my mum plays and the things she shows to me, over and over again. They used to belong to Marianne.

What I can't remember is myself.

It's just like the doctor says – I'm not here. I'm like a mirror. I reflect things – my mother, my teddy bear, my CDs, my clothes. But I am gone. I can't remember who Marianne was, how she used to feel or think. I can't remember her face. I can't remember anything about her. Marianne's body is here – her memories are here – but she is gone.

I only have a past. I have no present. I have no future.

I'd like to tell them that it's all right. Marianne would agree if she were here. She wouldn't want everyone to keep coming into the hospital for year after year, watching her getting older and older and older. So yes, please. Turn me off, pull out my tubes. I've done nothing but lie here for all this time and I'm still so, so tired. I just want it to stop.

Another month. Just one.

More than enough for me.

CHAPTER 6

Wake Up

MUM

Aidan and I clop along the corridors, people
on every side. We're carrying armfuls of
streamers and balloons and plastic boxes full
of sausage rolls and jelly and other party food.

Hospitals are always so quiet. Hush, people are ill, don't make any noise.

But today is different. Today Marianne is 15 years old. It's her birthday and she's going out with a bang.

The doctors didn't approve. "A party in a hospital?" they said. "Loud music? Friends, dancing? Well ... there are other people in here, you know. Sick people ..."

But the party makes me feel better.
We've got used to the idea that she's gone –
now we just want to celebrate her life.

"Happy birthday, Marianne! Goodbye,
darling. Look, Rory is here, and Nana and
Grandad and Jess and Zara."

They didn't let us bring Daisy the cat –
animals in the ward were just too much.
But everyone else is here. Who knows, if we
make enough noise, maybe we'll wake up the
dead.

You, I mean. Maybe we'll wake you up.

I open the door. There she is, her head
pushed back as always. All together now ...

"Happy Birthday, Marianne!"

CHAPTER 7

In the Mirror

MARIANNE

Happy Birthday, Marianne!

It was a good party. They all enjoyed themselves – well, they looked as if they did, anyway.

Now Mum and Dad are sitting on my bed, each holding one of my hands. There are streamers all over the bed, balloons rolling on the floor. They popped so many that the nurse came in and said we'd give the other patients a heart attack if we made any more noise.

There was a cake with candles, there was jelly and sausage rolls. We played the music so loud! Jess and Zara did a dance around the room and nearly knocked the heart monitor off its stand. Mum and Dad turned out the lights and lit the candles and everyone sang "Happy Birthday", and they all blew out the candles for Marianne.

Marianne would have enjoyed it. It's a pity she couldn't come.

Yes, I know. I've let you all down. I didn't dance or sing, I didn't even blink. But I did enjoy it. I wish I could say.

"Goodbye, darling. I'm so, so sorry. Goodbye."

"Goodbye, Marianne."

Yes. Goodbye, Mum, goodbye, Dad. It was good of you to try for so long. I'm sorry, but the doctor's right – Marianne isn't here. It's just this old shell and these old memories. They look the same, but they don't mean anything. Not really.

But poor old Mum, she has to try. One last time. Here she goes again, holding the things up before me.

Teddy bear, clothes, CDs. Picture of Marianne with her mum and dad. Picture of Marianne dancing with Jess and Zara.

Poor Marianne. Poor Mum and Dad! Tonight they take the tubes out. It won't hurt, they've told them that. It's the best thing.

Mum stands up. She puts the things back in the box by the side of the bed. She arranges the photos on the table by the bed. Marianne would be happy, but she's gone away, Mrs Sims. Honest. I'll give her your love if I see her where I'm going.

"We'd better go," she says.

Yes, Mum, go. It's all for the best.

My dad is saying "Let's go" too, but he isn't going. He has something in his hand.

"Worth a try," he says. "We haven't tried it for a while." And my dad moves something in front of me.

It's a mirror. At least, I think it's a mirror, but perhaps it's not. Because in the mirror is a picture of Marianne.

"Darling, look. It's you," Dad says.

It's Marianne.

"It's you, darling," he says again. "Marianne, can you see?"

No, it's not me. It's Marianne.

"Can you see, Marianne?"

Is it me? Is it me? Am I her?

CHAPTER 8

Do It Again

MARIANNE

"She moved, Julie. Look, she moved! Her mouth moved!"

I never move.

"Are you sure?" Mum says. "It's your imagination."

I can't blink, I can't move. I'm not here …

"She moved, I saw her!" Dad says.
"Marianne, do it again – look. Oh Lord, do it
again for your mother, darling. See, that's
you, that's you there in the mirror. Just
smile, darling, just do it again – oh, please,
please, I know I saw you … just try to smile,
Marianne."

Like this …

"Oh my God, she moved. She tried to
smile. Oh, God!" Mum is crying.

"Marianne! It's you!" Dad says. "It's you."

Is it really? Was that me all the time? Really? I never dreamed that was me …

Now Mum grabs hold of my hand.

"Squeeze, Marianne, squeeze hard if you can hear me."

And Dad's shouting and jumping around the room, and I want to cry too, because it really is me, you know. I saw it – I moved my mouth. I moved my mouth!

The door opens and the doctor comes in.

"What is it?" she asks.

"She moved," Mum and Dad cry out. "She tried to smile. She moved!"

"That's not possible."

The doctor comes to the bed and leans over into my face. My face. There is a long pause while I look around for the muscles. Where have they gone?

"Take her hand," Mum tells me. "Take her hand. Marianne, squeeze. Squeeze for the doctor. Marianne, please?"

I can feel the doctor's hand in mine.

I squeeze for dear life.